The Case of the Marshmallow Monster

Read all the Jigsaw Jones Mysteries

Coming Soon

The Case of the Marshmallow Monster

by James Preller
illustrated by Jamie Smith
cover illustration by R. W. Alley

A
LITTLE APPLE
PAPERBACK

SCHOLASTIC INC.
New York   Toronto   London   Auckland   Sydney
Mexico City   New Delhi   Hong Kong

For my camping buddies, Lisa, Nicholas, and Gavin.
And special thanks to my neighbors, Emily and David,
for teaching me the words to Mila's handclap rhyme.
—J. P.

Book design by Dawn Adelman

ISBN 0-439-18473-8

12 11 10 9 8 7 6 5 4 .   0 1 2 3 4 5/0

Printed in the U.S.A.   40
First Scholastic printing, July 2000

CONTENTS

Chapter One
Closed for Vacation

I hung a sign on my tree house. It read CLOSED FOR VACATION. If someone needed a detective, they'd be out of luck. Because Jigsaw Jones, private eye, was getting away from it all.

Let's face it. Nobody gets rich from detective work. Most kids earn their money by doing chores around the house. The chores aren't fun, and they aren't pretty. Like walking the dog, taking out the garbage, or even making the bed. I mean,

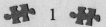

why bother making the bed? You're just going to *unmake* it later on.

That's why I became a detective. For a dollar a day, I make problems go away. It's good work. It's honest. You meet interesting people. And you never have to fold sheets.

But like I said, I needed a break.

Too bad I wasn't going to get one. I guess there's always somebody who needs a detective. Even on camping trips.

After all, missing marshmallows are a big problem.

And lake monsters are an even bigger problem. Yeesh.

It started on the first day of our third annual neighborhood camping trip. Every summer a group of fathers organizes it. This year we were going to Enchanted Lake State Campgrounds. My dad said it would be our best trip ever. Twenty-three kids were going, both boys and girls. We'd hike, swim, and play flashlight tag. We'd build roaring fires and sleep in tents. We'd toast marshmallows and eat s'mores until our stomachs hurt. S'mores are a sandwich made of graham crackers, a melted marshmallow, and a piece of chocolate.

Everyone wants to eat some more! That's why we call them s'mores.

Best of all, Shirley Hitchcock's dad

always told us spooky stories around the campfire. He scared us silly, then sent us off to bed. It was fun to lie awake under the stars, listening for creepy sounds in the night.

Oooooh.

Creeeeeeak.

Squish, squish, squish.

Deep down, we knew that Mr. Hitchcock's stories weren't true. There were no such things as forest monsters and bogeymen and killer porcupines.

Right?

Toot-toot. I heard my dad sound the car horn. It was time to leave. I raced to the front of the house. We all piled into the minivan. Mr. Jordan sat beside my dad in the front passenger seat. I sat squished between Joey Pignattano and Ralphie Jordan. My brothers Daniel and Nick were squeezed in the back with all the gear.

And they were complaining already.

 4

"Boys, we're still in the driveway," my dad said. "Could you hold off on the complaints until we get around the block?"

Nick protested, "But I've got a tent pole digging into my ribs!"

Nick was right. I'd seen sardines with more legroom.

"The campground is only two hours away," my dad replied. "You'll live." He put the car into reverse.

My mom waved good-bye from the driveway. "I'll miss you," she called. I wasn't too sure about that. She seemed happy to see us go.

Thrilled, in fact.

Go figure.

Chapter Two
A Tent with Hiccups

We got to the campground right on time. That is, if your idea of "right on time" includes a flat tire and getting lost in the middle of nowhere. That's the place right after my dad says, "I know a little shortcut."

It's a few miles past "I don't need a map."

Naturally, we were the last to arrive at the campground. After another hour, we finished setting up. I was going to share a tent with Ralphie and Joey. My brothers had their own tent.

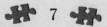

That's when I noticed the tent beside us. It wasn't a tent, exactly. It was more like a crumpled-up lump on the ground. I looked closer. It was moving.

And muttering.

Oof. Ouch. Hiccup. "What the . . . ?" *Hiccup.* "Heeelp. Er, I'm trapped. Get me outta this thing!"

Joey pointed. "I think it's alive."

"And it's got the hiccups," Ralphie noted.

I poked it with a stick. "Anybody in there?"

A voice answered. "Yes. It's me! Stringbean!" *Hiccup!* "I've been trapped in here for hours!"

Stringbean Noonan, I thought. That was a surprise. I didn't expect to see him here. Stringbean's real name was Jasper. And he wasn't the outdoor type.

"Hold on. Let me find the zipper," Ralphie said. He fumbled around for a moment. Then . . . *ziiiiiip.*

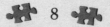

In a moment, Jasper crawled out, red-faced and sweaty. He kicked the heavy nylon tent. "That thing" — *hiccup!* — "nearly ATE me!"

We all laughed.

Joey discovered that Stringbean had forgotten one very important thing. Tent poles!

Stringbean shrugged. "Don't look at me," he replied. "I don't know anything about camping. I wouldn't even be here if my dad

didn't make me come. I'd rather be eating cheese puffs and watching Nickelodeon!"

Stringbean Noonan was the kind of kid who was afraid of his own shadow. He was afraid of bees, thunder, horses, lightning, and heights.

Now he could add something else to the list.

Tents.

The poor guy was afraid of tents.

Chapter Three
To Build a Fire

Our group had reserved twelve sites in the campground. Right away, the dads turned two sites into the cooking and eating areas. They carried over a bunch of picnic tables and put them in a U-shape. It looked really cool.

There was an open field across the way. Beyond that, a lake with a little sandy beach. We found my dad and Mr. Jordan by the cooking area. They were laughing, unloading food, and putting things in order.

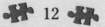

"Who's cooking tonight?" Ralphie asked.

"You're looking at him," my dad said.

Ralphie whispered to me, "I hope your dad is a better cook than driver. I thought we'd never get here."

My dad frowned. "I heard that, Ralphie. Never fear, Chef Jones is here! Spaghetti dinner tonight! I promise not to take a shortcut looking for the meatballs."

We told them about Stringbean's missing tent poles. Mr. Jordan knelt down in front of Stringbean. "Don't worry, Greenbean. We'll find a place for you to sleep."

Jasper mumbled, "It's Stringbean, sir."

Mr. Jordan looked confused. He couldn't understand Stringbean's mumble-jumble. "String cheese?" he asked. "Do you want a piece of string cheese?"

"Never mind," Stringbean said.

My dad spoke up. "You can sleep with Jigsaw's brothers Daniel and Nick. They have extra room in their tent."

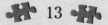

Mr. Jordan stood and pointed. "Ah, here comes everybody."

We saw a large group of kids walking toward us from the lake. They were wet and smiling. "You guys missed it!" Mila Yeh cried out. "The lake's awesome. Where have you been?"

Mila was my friend and partner. We did all our detective work together. Mila looked at us, then at my dad. "Don't tell me. Your dad got lost again."

"Lost?" my dad said. "Lost?! I wouldn't call it lost."

Mr. Jordan laughed. "What would you call it, then?"

My dad arched an eyebrow. "The scenic route," he replied. "Anyway, gather some wood, kids. We'll make a bonfire tonight. In the meantime, I'll start cooking."

After dinner, Lucy Hiller's father taught us how to build a "proper" fire. Then he

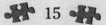

firmly told us we should never, ever build a fire.

I scratched my head and watched.

"You need three kinds of wood for a fire," Mr. Hiller explained. He held out a handful of pine needles, dry grasses, and wood shavings. "This is called tinder. It catches fire easily and burns fast."

He set a small pile in the fire area. "Next, we need kindling. These dry twigs will do nicely." He set them on top of the tinder in a little pyramid.

Mr. Hiller lit the tinder. A few small flames began to lick at the kindling. Mr. Hiller explained, "When the kindling catches, we'll add larger pieces of wood. Dead, dry sticks are best. There seem to be plenty lying around. Go find some, boys and girls. Remember, don't hurt any trees. Leave the living branches alone. I only want deadwood that's already on the ground."

After we gathered wood for the fire, it got

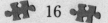

dark. A gang of us played flashlight tag in the field. Then it was story time. Mr. Hitchcock told the coolest, scariest stories. And along with it — we ate s'mores!

It was only the greatest food on the planet.

Chapter Four
Mr. Hitchcock Tells a Story

Mr. Hitchcock wasn't green. And he didn't have a stem growing out of his head. But other than that, he looked exactly like a pear. With arms and legs, naturally. Mr. Hitchcock had narrow shoulders and a wide stomach. His head was large and perfectly bald. His lower lip was thick and he didn't appear to have a neck.

He sat down with a heavy grunt. We all watched him closely. Four-year-old Sally-Ann Simms, who was the youngest kid on the trip, sat on the log between Mr.

 19

Hitchcock and Jasper Noonan. I liked Sally-Ann. She was a hurricane in lavender and pink. If you told Sally-Ann a scary story, she'd just shrug. Then she'd politely request, "More blood, please."

Mr. Hitchcock shivered. He said loudly to no one in particular, "Well, I talked to the ranger. She said everything's been quiet. No signs of the lake creature. So I think we'll be safe."

"Lake creature?" Danika Starling asked.

"Like, whoa. Back up. Did you say lake creature?"

"Oh, never mind," Mr. Hitchcock said. He glanced nervously in the direction of the lake. "It's probably nothing. I doubt the stories are true."

"What stories?" my brother Nick asked.

"Yeah, what stories?" piped up Wingnut O'Brien and his best friend, Freddy Fenderbank. Wingnut and Freddy were like peanut butter and jelly. You never saw one without the other. This was their first time on one of our camping trips.

Wingnut was my next-door neighbor. I didn't know much about Freddy. He had messy red hair and less than a million freckles. From the look of his clothes, I'd say he'd recently been attacked by a mud puddle.

Mr. Hitchcock stirred the fire with a long stick. He shifted uncomfortably in his seat. We sat gathered around the warm flames,

waiting. "I shouldn't have said anything," he muttered, scolding himself. "I don't want to scare you kids."

A chorus of voices went up.

"It's okay."

"We won't get scared."

"Besides, we like getting scared."

I noticed Jasper Noonan's face turning white. He didn't say a word.

Sally-Ann nodded enthusiastically. "Scare us!" she demanded.

Mr. Hitchcock sighed. "Well, maybe I

should tell you. But only for your safety."

Everyone sat perfectly still, hardly breathing. *WHOOOOOO*. An owl hooted from a distant tree. Mr. Hitchcock gazed into the night sky. A full moon gazed back. He sighed. "It began a few years ago," he said. "It was a misty night like tonight, full of shadows and dark gloom."

Mr. Hitchcock continued, "It's on full moons like tonight, you know, when the creature crawls out of the lake. He slips into the darkness and prowls around."

Chapter Five

Sweet Dreams

"What does the lake creature look like?" Ralphie asked.

"Hard to say," Mr. Hitchcock replied. "Some say it's eight feet tall and covered with scales. Some say it's dark green. Others say it's as black as night. Some say it's got claws. One man swears it's got webbed feet. They say it's afraid of light — fire and flashlights, mostly. But no one has gotten a real good look at the creature. In fact, only one person has seen it up close. And he's not talking anymore."

Danika Starling stood up, waving her arms. "Whoa, whoa, whoa," she said. "Not talking anymore? Like, you're not saying that he's . . ."

"Dead?" offered Mr. Hitchcock. He shook his head. "No, not dead. He's just *not talking anymore*. To anyone. He just lies in bed and stares at the ceiling. Too scared to even speak."

"Wh-wh-what happened to him?" Jasper stammered.

Mr. Hitchcock stabbed at the fire with his stick. Orange sparks flew into the sky. "No one knows for sure," he said. "It was late at night. The boy was camping right over there." He pointed. "Well, you know what they say about camping: *Never leave your tent at night without a flashlight.*

"Well, this boy didn't listen. He had to use the bathroom. But he forgot his flashlight. That's probably when he ran into the lake creature." Mr. Hitchcock shook his head sadly. "The poor, poor child."

A chilling cry broke the silence. *Hooooowl. A-oooooo.* Mr. Hitchcock turned sharply, listening. "Coyotes," he murmured. "Just coyotes."

Then he stood, rubbing his hands together. "Don't worry, kids," he cheerfully announced. "The creature won't bother

 26

you. Just keep quiet. Stay in your tents. Everything will be fine."

"Wh-wh-why does it prowl around?" Freddy asked.

Mr. Hitchcock rubbed the top of his bald head. "Food," he whispered. "The creature loves human food."

Freddy gulped.

Mila swallowed hard.

Jasper sneezed.

Nicole wheezed.

And Sally-Ann shouted, "PLEASE! Tell us more!"

Mr. Jordan interrupted the story. "I'd say that's enough for tonight, Alfred. It's time these kids got ready for bed." Mr. Jordan pointed at me and a few others. "Come with me, kids. I've got a job for you."

We followed Mr. Jordan to the cooking area. He lit a kerosene lamp and handed Ralphie a large garbage bag. "I want this area spotless," he said. "Not a single crumb. Hungry animals live in these woods — including black bears. Leaving food out is an invitation for trouble."

"Would a bear come into camp?" Mila asked.

Mr. Jordan ran his fingers over his mustache. "If you left food out? Absolutely. They love a free meal. But a raccoon is much more likely. Those little rascals are real scavengers."

Ralphie chimed in, "That's why raccoons wear black masks! They steal food!"

Mr. Jordan chuckled. Then he left us alone to clean up.

Danika came up beside me. "Do you believe in the lake creature?" she asked.

I shrugged. "I don't know. Maybe. It might be true. Like Bigfoot."

Danika shivered. "To think I went swimming in that lake today. Whoa. That's, like, *sooooo* not cool."

Wingnut O'Brien stared at the cleaned-up site. He looked worried. "What if the lake creature comes — and there's no food?"

"He'll still be hungry," Joey said. "For human food."

"And he'll want to eat one of us!" Ralphie joked. "Bwaa-ha-ha."

"Don't joke around," Danika scolded. "You're creeping me out."

"Let's leave some food out for it," suggested Joey. "Just a little snack."

"No way!" Mila cried. "You heard Mr. Jordan. Food is an invitation for trouble."

We took a vote. Only Mila and Danika voted against it. Sally-Ann grabbed a bag of marshmallows. "The lake creature will love these," she said, handing me the bag.

Mila sighed. "I have a bad feeling about this, Jigsaw. A very bad feeling." Mila felt a little better when we put the bag at the edge of the woods, near a pile of rocks. "At

least now the creature won't wander into the center of camp," she reasoned.

Before zipping up our tent for the night, we saw my father checking the area. He was carrying a garbage bag and a flashlight. He wore a blanket wrapped around his shoulders. "Good night, boys," he called kindly. "Sweet dreams."

Yeah. Sure. Sweet dreams.

Sour nightmares was more like it.

Lake creatures.

Yeesh.

Chapter Six

A Secret Message

"Jigsaw, Ralphie, wake up!"

Morning. Ugh. I tried to lift my eyelids. It might have been easier to lift a piano with my pinkie.

Joey was urgently whispering, "The marshmallows are gone!"

Ralphie snapped awake. "It's real. The lake creature is real!"

Camp was soon buzzing with the news. It's all anyone talked about over pancakes and orange juice. Everybody was scared and excited. The story kept getting bigger

and bigger. And now the lake creature had a new name.

The Marshmallow Monster!

After breakfast, I found a note on my sleeping bag.

HOW	BARK		APE	
SEEK	SWIM			
	DIRT	SEEN		
	LIKE	EAT		
TOOTH	A	FLOWER		
BAT	TALK			
VERY	BIG	CAR		
BEAR	IS	BLACK		
BUT	IS			
NOT	SLEEPING			

The note was from Mila. She always tested my brainpower with secret codes. I inspected the paper. It had been folded twice, leaving heavy crease marks. I noticed that certain letters landed on the creases. I took out a yellow marker and drew a line down the creases.

That's it, I thought. It's a crease code. The trick was to start with folded paper. Then Mila wrote the message in the creases of the paper. None of the other letters mattered.

I quickly figured it out. WE HAVE A NEW CASE.

I found Mila down by the lake. She was sitting across from Danika Starling. They were singing a handclap rhyme.

"Chicka-chicka, boom-boom.
I can do karate!
Chicka-chicka, boom-boom.
I can move my body!
Chicka-chicka, boom-boom.
I won't tell my mommy!
Chicka-chicka, boom-boom.
Oops, I'm sorry!"

At "Oops," they pushed each other on the forehead and giggled.

"What's up?" I said.

"Danika wants to hire us," Mila explained.

I frowned at Danika. Dark rings circled her eyes, like she didn't get enough sleep last night. I shook my head. "Sorry, closed for vacation. I'm not taking any cases."

"What do you mean, you're not taking any cases?" Danika said.

"Just what it sounds like," I replied. "I've been working too hard lately."

Danika's eyes narrowed. "You're afraid, aren't you?"

I answered with a long, slow yawn.

I looked around. It was a perfect day. That is, if you go for blue sky and sunshine. The lake was empty. A lone lifeguard sat staring into space. "How come no one's swimming?" I asked.

Danika put her hands on her hips. "Like, duh. With that lake creature out there? No way anyone's going in that water!"

I nodded. "Why take chances, right?"

"Right," Danika said.

Don't ask why I did what I did. Because I'm not even sure myself. I slipped off my sneakers and socks. I pulled off my shirt. And walked into the lake.

"Jigsaw! What are you doing?!" Mila cried.

"Swimming," I answered. I dove headfirst

into the murky black water. The lake felt cool against my body. I swam out a little farther. Then farther.

"Come back, Jigsaw," Danika urged. "The lake creature!"

I called back, "I'm not afraid of any lake creature."

That's when I felt it.

Something brushed against my leg.

Something slithery.

Like weeds. Or a fish. Or a snake.

Or a . . . *finger.*

I kicked my leg away. My feet strained to touch bottom. They reached, barely. The bottom was gooey, like mud. For a brief moment, my feet felt stuck. Not like mud, I thought. Like quicksand! A wave of fear washed over me.

Then I felt it again.

Something scratching against my skin.

Something was in the lake with me.

Something I couldn't see.

I kicked my legs free and raced for shore. When I reached the beach, I bent over, panting hard.

"Wow, you're a fast swimmer," Danika observed.

I stared at her blankly. "I've changed my mind," I gasped, still puffing hard. "I'll take the case."

No lake creature was going to make a monkey out of me.

Chapter Seven
Piecing the Clues Together

When I need to think, I do jigsaw puzzles. It's like solving mysteries. Each piece is a little clue. All you've got to do is put it together, piece by piece.

Unfortunately, I didn't pack any puzzles for the trip. After all, I was on vacation. I didn't plan on thinking. But I did bring some markers and my detective journal. I never left home without them.

I turned to a clean page and wrote, The Case of the Marshmallow Monster. Beneath that, I wrote, Client: Danika Starling.

Under Crime I wrote, Stolen Marshmallows.

I wrote the word Clues. I underlined it. I chewed on my marker and tried to think. The chewing didn't help get my brain started. It didn't do much for the marker, either. I didn't have a clue. But I did have a suspect. Unfortunately, it lived in the lake and tickled swimmers for laughs.

I drew a picture of the lake creature. It was so good I nearly scared myself.

Ziiiiiip. A noise from behind startled me. Joey Pignattano climbed into the tent. His knee landed hard on my ankle. "Hey, Jigsaw," he asked. "You don't have any ginger ale, do you?"

"No," I replied. "Look in the coolers by the picnic tables. Maybe in there."

Joey turned to leave. This time, he crushed my foot. "Sorry, Jigsaw!" he apologized. "I didn't mean to step on your foot."

"That's okay, Joey. I walk on it, too."

"Huh?" Joey said.

I watched as my little joke sailed over his head, out of the tent, into the clear sky beyond. "Never mind," I grunted. "Why do you want ginger ale, anyway?"

"Wingnut and Freddy have stomachaches. I figured some ginger ale might help them feel better," Joey said.

"Too many s'mores?" I wondered.

Joey made a face. "Too many s'mores? Impossible! There's never enough." Then he left to look for ginger ale. That's Joey for you. Just an all-around nice guy.

I closed my notebook. Mr. Hiller was leading a hike to a nearby waterfall. I

wanted to go. But I had a picture of George Washington in my pocket. His face was on the dollar bill Danika gave me. Someone — *or something* — was stealing marshmallows. George said it was my job to find out who and try to stop him.

Even if it's a monster.

Covered with green slime.

Who prowls in the night.

Next vacation, I promised myself, I'm going to Disney World.

OFFICE

Chapter Eight
More Suspects

"So, this is your office, huh," Mila said.

"That's what the sign says," I replied. I'd spent the last half hour putting a bunch of sticks on the ground. They spelled out O-F-F-I-C-E.

"Some office," Mila teased. "It looks like a big rock to me."

"Hey, give me a break," I said. "It *is* a big rock. You have to use your imagination. Did you find any clues by the lake?"

Mila shook her head. "Nope. No strange footprints. Not a single sign of the lake

creature. To tell you the truth," she said, "I'm not convinced it's real."

I thought about my swim in the lake. When I closed my eyes, I could still feel it: that thing scratching at my legs. I showed Mila a page in my journal. "We've got a long list of suspects."

SUSPECTS
＊ Lake Creature
＊ Black bear
＊ Raccoon
＊ Squirrel
＊ Joey Pignattano
＊ Ralphie Jordan
＊ Danika Starling
＊ Freddy Fenderbank
＊ Wingnut O'Brien
＊ Sally-Ann Simms
＊ Stringbean Noonan

I pointed to the bottom half of the list. "These people were all there when we put out the marshmallows. That makes them suspects."

Mila nodded silently, thinking. She crossed her arms and rocked back and forth. "Danika slept in the tent with me. She never left. It couldn't be her."

I drew a line through Danika's name.

"What about Joey?" I asked. "He had the opportunity."

"But he discovered the missing marshmallows," Mila protested.

"Exactly," I replied. "Joey got up when we were all asleep. He could have eaten the marshmallows, then lied about it."

Mila pulled on her long black hair. She snapped her fingers. "Joey ate six pancakes this morning. That's a lot. He couldn't have eaten a bag of marshmallows, too."

"Are you kidding?" I snorted. "Joey will eat anything, anytime, anywhere. This is

 48

a guy who once ate a worm for a dollar. When it comes to eating, Joey is the Energizer Bunny. He never stops."

Mila nodded. "Okay. He's still a suspect."

I moved further down the list. "Ralphie never left the tent." I crossed out his name.

"Stringbean?" Mila asked.

"Doubt it," I said. "He doesn't like the dark. But I'll check with my brothers to make sure."

That left three names: Sally-Ann, Wingnut, and Freddy.

"Sally-Ann shared a tent with Shirley Hitchcock," Mila said. "I'll see what I can find out."

"I'll talk to Wingnut and Freddy," I said. "But let's check the scene of the crime first. There might be clues."

We walked over together. "I hope it wasn't one of our friends," Mila said. "I hate when that happens."

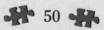

"Yeah, but it beats having a hungry bear wandering around our camp," I replied.

Mila laughed. "That's it! All we've got to do is find a bear with a stomachache!"

I stopped. "What did you say?"

"It was a joke," Mila explained. "If a bear ate all those marshmallows, he wouldn't be feeling too well."

I remembered Joey's search for ginger ale. I thought about Wingnut and Freddy. And I suddenly had a lot of questions rattling around my head. And each question needed an answer. Just like cookies needed milk.

Chapter Nine

The Confession

The scene of the crime was a bust. "It hasn't rained in a while," Mila said, frowning. "The ground is hard. There aren't many tracks."

I examined a patch of dirt. I didn't find any webbed footprints. I did discover some sneaker prints, but that was no big deal. We'd all tramped around there last night.

"There's no empty marshmallow bag," Mila noticed. "That's strange. An animal wouldn't eat plastic. But it wouldn't throw it away, either."

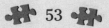

"Maybe it blew away," I suggested. "Maybe the creature took the whole bag. Maybe it ate the marshmallows somewhere else."

Mila's lips tightened. "Maybe," she said.

We decided to split up. Mila went to check on Sally-Ann Simms. I had to find out about Stringbean.

I talked to my brothers. They said that Stringbean spent the night zipped inside his sleeping bag — head and all! Nick shook his head sadly. "He was scared to death, Jigsaw. Stringbean kept mumbling about lake monsters. He said he'd rather be eating cheese puffs and watching Nickelodeon."

"Weird kid," Daniel observed.

No kidding. I crossed Jasper's name off the list. That left Wingnut and Freddy. I found them sitting by the edge of the lake. They were skipping rocks in the water.

"Feeling better?" I asked.

Wingnut shot a look at Freddy. Freddy stared at the ground. Wingnut nervously pulled on his ear. Freddy kicked a rock. "Er, sure," Wingnut stammered. "We feel fine."

Freddy bobbed his head up and down. Like he really, really agreed with Wingnut. It was funny watching them. They weren't very good at lying.

"I heard you guys were sick this morning. What was the matter? Too many marshmallows?"

Wingnut pulled on his ear. Freddy bit his lip. Both stared at the ground.

"Look, guys," I said. "Let's not play games. You took the marshmallows, didn't you?"

"Took the marshmallows?! No way!" Wingnut protested. He looked directly into my eyes. "Honest, Jigsaw. We didn't touch the marshmallows."

I believed him. Wingnut didn't pull on his ear or look away. Instead, his eyes met mine. But something was still wrong. "Explain the stomachaches," I demanded.

Freddy and Wingnut exchanged looks. "We can't," Wingnut said. "We might get into trouble."

That wasn't good enough for me. I wanted facts. And I wasn't leaving without them.

Freddy finally broke down and confessed. "Please don't tell anyone, Jigsaw," he pleaded. "I know we weren't supposed to bring candy into our tents. But . . ."

 56

"Candy?" I repeated.

"Yeah," Wingnut said, smiling at the memory. "A jumbo package of Reese's peanut butter cups. We ate them all!"

"Six each," Freddy said proudly.

"We felt pretty sick," Wingnut admitted. "But it was worth it."

I crossed their names off the list. "Don't worry, guys. I won't say a word."

I was still laughing to myself when I ran into Danika Starling. The afternoon

light was fading fast. "Did you find the marshmallow monster?" she asked.

"Tonight," I promised.

Danika's eyes widened. "Tonight? That's, like, *soooo* cool!"

"Yeah, it's like that," I replied.

"So what's your plan?" she asked.

"Night surveillance," I said.

"Surveillance? What's that?" Danika asked.

"It's watching without being seen," I answered.

"Oh, spying," Danika said. "Can I come with you?"

I shook my head. "Too dangerous. It's something I have to do alone."

Danika took off her necklace. She handed it to me. I saw that it was a leather string with a whistle attached. "You might need it," she said. "You know how to whistle, don't you? You just put your lips together and blow."

Chapter Ten

Waiting in the Dark

Shirley Hitchcock said that Sally-Ann Simms snored through the night. We crossed her name off the list. Besides monsters and wild animals, Joey was the last suspect left.

During s'mores, I placed another bag of marshmallows in the same spot as before. I made sure Joey knew about it, too.

The trap was set.

Together, Mila and I picked a spot for me to hide in. It was a few feet past the clearing, into the forest. It was behind a huge

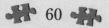

oak tree, not far from the marshmallows. I could see the entire campground from there. Hopefully, no one could see me.

I waited until Joey and Ralphie were fast asleep. Then I carefully climbed out of the tent. I slowly, slowly zipped it back up, cringing at the sound. No one woke. I reached into my pocket and took the little bell that I'd borrowed from Sally-Ann Simms. I tied it to the outside zipper.

If Joey left the tent, I'd hear ringing in my

ears. I didn't want to believe that he was the marshmallow monster. But I had to make sure.

Each tent had its own flashlight. I took ours just in case. But I didn't turn it on. I cautiously picked my way through the darkness. Finally I reached the tree. *Hooooowl. A-oooooo.* I trembled. "Just coyotes," I told myself.

There I sat and waited. Alone in the dark. Because that's what detectives do. We sit. We watch. And we wait. Sooner or later, something happens. It always does.

Only tonight, I was hoping for the opposite. I wanted a nice, quiet evening. A night when nothing happens. I fingered the whistle in my pocket. The air was cool. A slight breeze kicked up. Branches shivered. I watched as the moon, like a cold white eye, looked down upon me.

Night settled around me. And with it, the noises of the night. Crickets chittered.

Branches moaned in the wind. An owl screeched. And then, behind me, I heard small feet scampering to safety.

Fears swirled through my brain. Every sound became a footstep. Every shadow became a monster. I slowly grew tired, so very tired. I had trouble keeping my eyes open. I must have fallen asleep. I dreamed of lake creatures and bears. Raccoons and wolves.

I never heard a sound. I suddenly felt something grab my shoulder. . . .

Shake me . . .

"Huh? What?"

"Jigsaw, Jigsaw! It's me!"

A voice in my dream seemed to be whispering to me from far, far away. . . .

"It's me! Mila."

I gazed wildly into the forest. My eyes struggled to make out the shape hovering beside me. Slowly, I saw the whiteness of her teeth, her eyes.

 64

"You were sleeping," Mila said softly. "I've come to stay with you."

I didn't argue. I was glad for the company.

We sat in silence for five minutes. Ten minutes. Fifteen minutes.

Then a branch snapped. Loud and near. *Crack.*

Mila squeezed my arm.

"Shhhh. It's coming this way."

Chapter Eleven

Oops

Crunch, crunch, crunch. Steps in the dirt, kicking stones, crushing leaves.

Then they stopped. Slowly got softer, more distant. The steps were moving away from us.

Tinkle, tinkle.

The bell, faint as a whisper! It came from the other direction. "It's Joey," I whispered to Mila. "He must be up."

But we again heard the footsteps coming closer, closer. I realized that the steps were coming . . . from the lake. I remembered Mr.

Hitchcock's words: *The creature crawls out of the lake . . . and prowls around.*

I aimed the flashlight at the footsteps. But I didn't dare turn it on. Not now, not yet. I wanted to remain hidden in the secret dark.

My eyes darted to the pile of rocks. The marshmallows were untouched. I strained to see my tent through the blur of night. "We should have seen him by now," I whispered to Mila. "Joey must have gone the other way, to the bathroom."

"I hope he took a flashlight," Mila whispered back.

Again Mr. Hitchcock's warning came to my ears. *Never leave your tent without a flashlight.*

No, I thought to myself. No, no, no. I had taken the flashlight. I had it in my hand! That meant Joey was wandering around in the dark.

Alone.

Crunch, crunch, snap.

Not alone, I thought. Worse than alone. Much worse. It was out there. The creature.

"Look!" Mila whispered, her voice filled with fear.

It was a hulking shape. Tall and dark and thick. Walking, stopping, bending, stopping. Lumbering toward us. No, toward the marshmallows.

I squeezed Mila's hand. "Grab a stone," I told her. "Ready?"

I felt her nod — a sharp jerk of the head. She was ready. "One, two, three . . . NOW!"

We jumped up and screamed. We threw stones at the creature's body. I blew the whistle. *Tweeet! Twee-tweeeet!*

"What the . . . ? Ouch! Who threw that? WHO'S OUT THERE?!"

The camp swarmed in chaos. At the scream of the whistle, everyone leaped out of their sleeping bags. Voices shouted,

zippers unzipped. People came running, tripping, fumbling in the dark.

I aimed my flashlight at the creature.

And there stood . . . my father.

Oops.

He was rubbing a small bruise on his arm.

And he was not a happy camper.

It took a while to sort things out. At first, my dad was pretty mad. But after I explained things, he understood. Sort of. In a "still angry" kind of way.

He said that he checked the campground every night, making sure everything was in order. "I make sure there's no food left out accidentally," he said. "That's what happened with your marshmallows last night. I found them."

"You ate them?" Mila asked.

"No, Mila," my dad said. "I picked them up and put them in the car . . . where they belong." He glared at me. But he couldn't

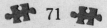

keep it up. Slowly, a broad grin crossed his face. He touched the bruise on his arm.

"Does it hurt?" I asked.

He shook his head. "I'll be fine."

Sally-Ann Simms stomped over. "You mean there's no monster?" she asked.

"No monster," my father answered.

"Bummer!" Sally-Ann stormed back to her tent.

Nick and Daniel were impressed. They looked at my dad's bruise. "Nice aim," they said.

"Hey, where's Stringbean?" I asked.

Nick grinned. "Still in his sleeping bag. I don't think he's ever coming out."

"Nice work, detective." It was Danika, smiling brightly. "Thanks. Now I can go swimming again!"

Well, it wasn't exactly the vacation I had

hoped for. I had wanted peace and quiet. Instead, I got marshmallows and monsters.

But if you ask me, vacations are overrated. I prefer a good mystery any day of the week!